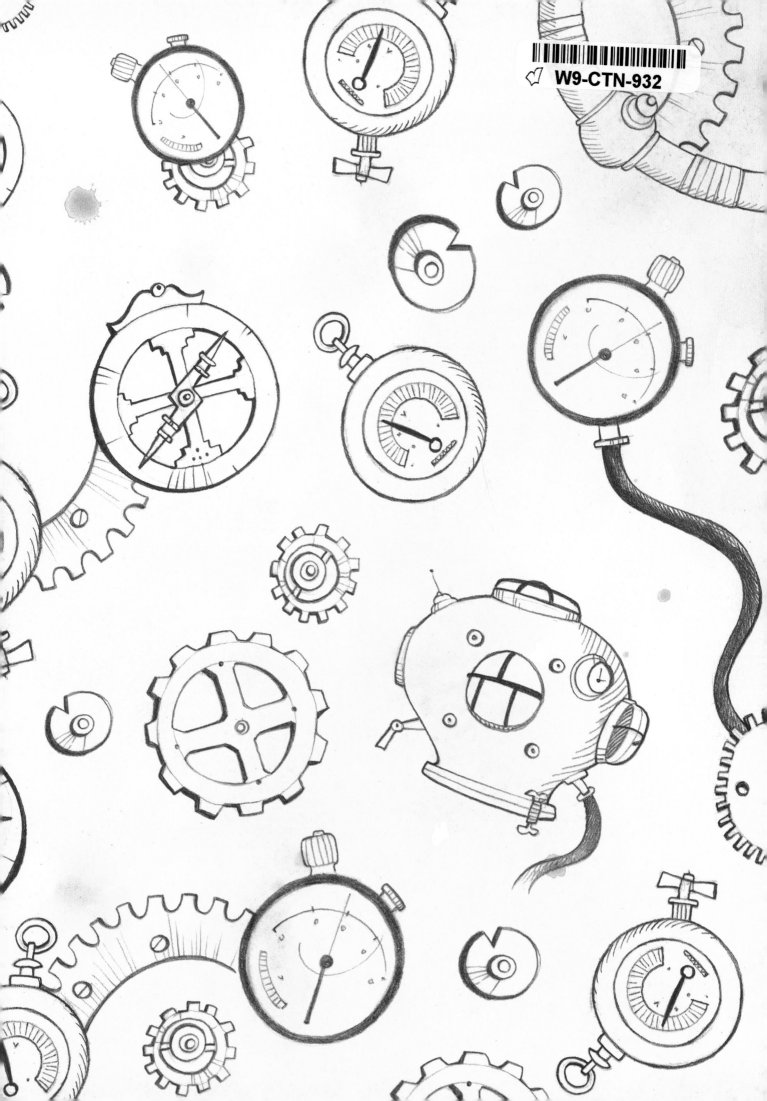

Twenty Thousand Leagues Under the Sea

from the masterpiece by
Jules Verne

illustrations by
Francesca Rossi

WHITE STAR KIDS

days. To my great joy, I was invited to join the search expedition.

The newspapers had been speaking of nothing but the mysterious and often-sighted sea monster for

The year 1866 was marked by disturbing news from seas the world over. For some time past, ships had been sighting a strange, mysterious creature – occasionally phosphorescent and larger and faster than any previously-known whale.

The newspapers spoke of nothing but this strange creature:

"It's a cetacean of unheard-of dimensions," some people said.

"It's no whale – so it has to be a monster," claimed others.

All trace of the mysterious creature was soon lost, until a series of inexplicable events began to occur: ships would collide with rocks unmarked on any nautical chart, or would suffer perfectly symmetrical gashes in the shape of a triangle on their sides.

I myself was in the United States during this period, on a scientific assignment on behalf of the Paris Museum of Natural History where I taught as a professor. As a naturalist and marine biologist, I had been following the bizarre occurrences with great interest. And, having published a volume entitled *The Mysteries of the Great Ocean Depths*, I was approached by the *New York Herald* to share my views on the matter. On the strength of the information available to us, I conjectured the existence of a giant narwhal, or sea unicorn.

Meanwhile, several governments were calling for a solution to ensure the safety of international waters. Thus an expedition was assembled to hunt down the monster, and when Commander Farragut was ready to set sail, I received the following telegram:

"Professor Aronnax, we would be pleased to welcome you on board the *Abraham Lincoln*."

"Conseil!" I called out impatiently. Conseil was my manservant, who accompanied me on all my journeys. "Did Master summon me?"

"Yes, my lad. Get our things ready – we depart immediately!"

"As Master wishes."

We reached the wharf in the blink of an eye, and had no sooner boarded the ship than Commander Farragut gave orders to cast off.

The *Abraham Lincoln* set off at full steam towards the treacherous waters of the Pacific Ocean, where the enormous creature had last been sighted. Determined to find the monster and free the seas once and for all, Commander Farragut had equipped his frigate with all the gear needed – including a cannon! – to capture the giant cetacean.

But, even more importantly, he had surrounded himself with uncommonly brave people like Ned Land, a harpooner who had no equal in his trade.

His harpoon never missed its target.

Canadian by birth, Ned Land was a tall, well-built man, fairly taciturn and not very sociable, who took an immediate liking to me. Little by little, he began telling tales of his adventures in the polar seas, his hunting expeditions and battles. But he never mentioned the mysterious creature we were hunting. He was the only man on board to not believe in it.

"How can you – of all people – doubt the existence of this enormous, astonishingly powerful cetacean we're after, Ned? A world-renowned whaler who has seen and fought against giant mammals his whole life..."

"That's the point, Professor – I've come across countless whales and other giant marine mammals, but no matter how large and fierce they were, none could come close to breaking through the iron plates of a steamer. Unless, as you say, this creature really does possess a strength as yet unheard of…" replied Ned, still unconvinced.

Meanwhile, the frigate continued its sea voyage undisturbed. After sailing along the eastern coast of South America, the *Abraham Lincoln* reached Cape Horn; after doubling the headland, we would finally reach Pacific waters.

"Keep your eyes open from now on!" were the commander's orders.

The ocean had never had so many eyes and spyglasses trained on it. Day and night, we carefully monitored its waters, and sailors crowded the masts until sundown, hanging onto each other as they scanned the horizon.

Thus, after crossing the Tropic of Capricorn and – soon after – the equator, our frigate veered westward and headed for the seas of the central Pacific, where the monster had last been sighted. We then explored the northern seas, the coasts of America and Japan. But after three months of sailing, we had found nothing – no sightings of giant narwhals or other cetaceans of indescribable size; no unknown sea "monsters", no underwater islands or colossal shipwrecks.

The crew began to lose heart, as disbelief in the existence of the supposed monster set in. In spite of the commander's perseverance, it soon became clear that the expedition couldn't last much longer. The *Abraham Lincoln* and its men had done all they could, and had nothing to reproach themselves with. By then off the shores of Japan, Commander Farragut was ready to order a turnabout towards European seas when we suddenly heard a shout from Ned Land:

"Ahoy, leeward! There it is!"

The entire crew – commander, sailors, cabin boys and all – rushed towards Ned.

Little by little, as the frigate moved forward, we noticed how the sea seemed to be lit up from underneath. My heart beat faster as we advanced slowly towards the glow.

Without a doubt, we were in the presence of the so-called "monster", which seemed to be moving towards us under water.

"Watch out! It's coming at us!"

"Weather the helm!" ordered Commander Farragut. "Reverse engines!" These orders were relayed immediately to the engine room, and the *Abraham Lincoln* described a semicircle, veering loudly and with great difficulty.

"Right your helm! Engines forward!" the commander called out.

hours awaiting this moment, harpoon in hand – was the first to spot it.

After an exhausting night of uncertainty, the "creature" approached at dawn. Ned – who had spent

As his orders were executed, the frigate moved away from the source of light. But not by much, as the creature soon followed in our wake, coming swiftly at us and circling around the vessel. We stood mute and motionless, gasping at what we saw. All of a sudden, the animal dashed towards us once more, stopping abruptly a few feet away.

Its glow died out all at once, and we had lost track of the creature when it suddenly reappeared on the other side of the ship – whether by circling around us again or gliding under the keel, we couldn't tell. So the commander gave the order to retreat, choosing to flee the monster rather than pursue it. "We don't know what kind of creature we're up against, and I don't want to run any risks in the darkness. We must act cautiously; let's wait for daylight to attack," he shouted, proving himself, once again, a wise and prudent man.

The crew stayed on their feet all night long: no one could even think of sleeping, with the thought of that unknown threat before us! The *Abraham Lincoln* had slowed down, with the monstrous creature following its example, and the state of affairs remained thus stalled for several hours. The glowing oval-shaped spot reappeared in the dead of night, however, not far from us. On the alert once more, we prepared for a battle at daylight.

Just as on the previous day, we heard Ned Land's shout: "Our enemy is behind us, on the port side!"

Turning to look in that direction, we saw a long, blackish body emerge from the waves, leaving an immense white wake behind.

"Stoke the furnaces, and full steam ahead!" ordered Farragut.

The frigate headed straight for the animal, but after three quarters of an hour, hadn't gained on the great cetacean at all.

"Keep the pressure mounting!" cried the commander.

The engineers obeyed his new order, stoking the furnaces at the risk of blowing us all sky-high.

The creature let us approach several times, only to accelerate, leaving us behind. Finally, however, Ned – who had stayed at his post the whole time, harpoon in hand – shouted: "There it is!"

Though the Canadian didn't believe the "creature" to be a giant cetacean, he had decided to tackle it the only way his experience in whaling had taught him.

He therefore grasped his harpoon and got ready to launch it.

But the whole morning went by in an endless chase: no sooner would Ned Land lean back to gather the necessary force to strike, than the giant narwhal would suddenly speed up, stealing away from us!

Towards noon, Commander Farragut decided he had had enough; no one could hold him and his crew in check! So he decided to use more drastic methods, and ordered his men to prepare the cannon.

The first shot passed some feet above the narwhal, while a second reached its target… but bounced off the beast's rounded back and fell into the sea.

"*Blast!*" The curse echoed among the members of the crew.

The *Abraham Lincoln* fought valiantly, but the creature it was struggling against was apparently as tireless as it was strong.

Meanwhile, night fell, cloaking the ocean in shadows. By then, I was sure that our expedition had come to an end, as had our hopes of ever seeing the fantastic animal again. But I was wrong! The unexpected occurred just a few minutes later: the intense light reappeared, just like the night before.

The narwhal – though I kept wondering how a cetacean could emit such a bright light – seemed motionless, and Farragut decided to take advantage of this. We advanced cautiously, fearful of awakening the beast.

All was silent on board. From my spot, I could see Ned Land grasping a rope in one hand, the other brandishing his dreaded harpoon. We were just a few feet from the creature. Ned Land launched his harpoon without warning, and we heard its resounding collision against the animal's hard body.

The light suddenly went out, and two waterspouts crashed down onto our frigate, sweeping over us.

I lost my balance as the ship toppled and, unable to find anything to hold onto, I was thrown overboard.

Though immediately dragged under water, I somehow managed to resurface, and began looking around for the frigate. It was pitch black out, and all I could see was a dark mass drifting away from me. Terrified, I began to shout as I floundered in a desperate attempt to reach the *Abraham Lincoln*.

"Help! Help!" I cried, struggling and panting. All of a sudden, I felt myself grabbed by a strong hand.

"Conseil! Conseil, my lad, is that you?! Were you also thrown overboard in the collision?"

"I dove after, Master, in the hopes of saving you. But, just as I jumped overboard, I heard the helmsman shouting that the rudder had been smashed."

"So the ship can no longer be steered… This means we're lost, Conseil."

"I'm afraid so, Master."

We decided to save our strength by taking turns swimming: while one of us would lie on his back, the other would propel him forward.

Our only hope of salvation was to wait for the lifeboat the *Abraham Lincoln* would surely send after us, once the frigate had recovered from the tremendous collision.

Though the sea was, luckily for us, quite calm, exhaustion overtook us after several hours. Our muscles stiffened with cramps as we began gasping for breath.

Calling out with the last of our strength, we thought we heard an answer to our plea for help.

Clinging to that voice, we began swimming towards it, still shouting though by now we were completely worn out.

Finally, the moon, peeping out from behind the clouds, shone down upon a familiar figure.

"Ned!" I shouted joyfully.

The Canadian pulled us out of the water with strong arms.

"Were you also thrown into the sea in the collision?"

"Not exactly into the sea, Professor; I landed on a floating islet."

"A floating islet? Explain yourself, Ned."

"Well, in other words… on the monster itself, Professor. All I know is that I landed on a plate of steel, which explains why my harpoon couldn't pierce it."

Right away, I tested the surface with my hands, and then with my foot. Sure enough, I found it to be a hard, impenetrable substance – not at all a soft-bodied marine mammal. "It's almost as if we've landed on the deck of some sort of submarine!" I exclaimed in astonishment. "Which means there must be an engine below us, and a crew to run it," I continued, looking at my companions. But Ned told us he had been on that surface for hours, and nothing had stirred. So we began searching for an opening that would allow us to communicate with whoever was inside but soon had to give up, in spite of our best efforts, as the surface, appeared smooth and flat all over. A few hours later, though, the strange object began to pick up speed, and we held on for dear life to a mooring ring we came across by chance. We remained in that unstable condition for several minutes, until we finally heard clanking noises from within. A platform was raised, and a man appeared.

Eight more men appeared silently after the first, and dragged us down into the mysterious object.

As the steel hatch closed over our heads, we found ourselves surrounded by darkness.

"What the devil…" exclaimed the whaler furiously. "Hospitality my foot! We may as well have ended up among pirates or cannibals! Well, I'm ready to put up a fight!"

"Calm down, Ned," I said quietly. "Don't be so irritable, and above all, don't do anything foolish. Why don't we try to find out where we are, instead?"

After half an hour had gone by, our prison finally lit up.
Rubbing our eyes, which had become used to the dark,
we looked around curiously and discovered ourselves
to be in a rather sparsely-furnished cabin.

There was no door to be seen, and all was quiet, but I was
sure the light had come on for a reason, and we were not left
to wonder for long.

We heard the sounds of a door being unbolted, then saw it open
and two men come in. One was short and stocky, while the
other was the most unusual-looking man I had ever seen. His
expression was one of strength and courage, but what struck
me most were his piercing black eyes. The latter of the two –
presumably the leader – observed us carefully without saying
a word. Then he turned to his companion, speaking with him
in a language I had never heard.

I spoke to him in French, telling the tale of our adventures
without omitting a single detail. When I was finished, however,
the man didn't pronounce a single word, nor did he give any
sign that he had understood my story.

Ned then told the same story in English, and Conseil in German;
in the end, I even tried to set down the facts in Latin, but all to
no avail.

Following this last attempt, the two strangers withdrew, leaving
us alone once more. But the door reopened soon after, and a
steward entered. He brought us some clothes and underclothes,
and set the table as we were changing into them. We sat down
to eat some well-cooked fish. Each utensil and plate bore the
letter N – perhaps the initial of the mysterious individual in
command of this strange submarine.

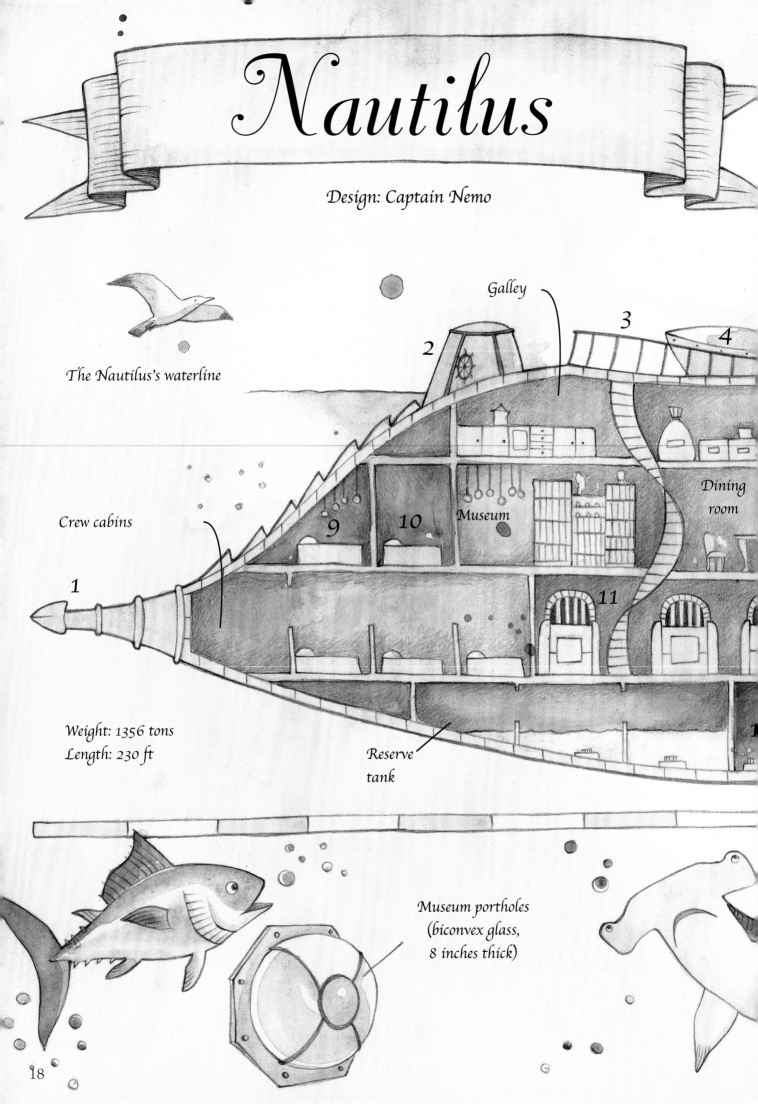

Nautilus

Design: Captain Nemo

Galley

The Nautilus's waterline

2

3

4

Crew cabins

9

10

Museum

Dining room

1

11

Weight: 1356 tons
Length: 230 ft

Reserve tank

Museum portholes
(biconvex glass,
8 inches thick)

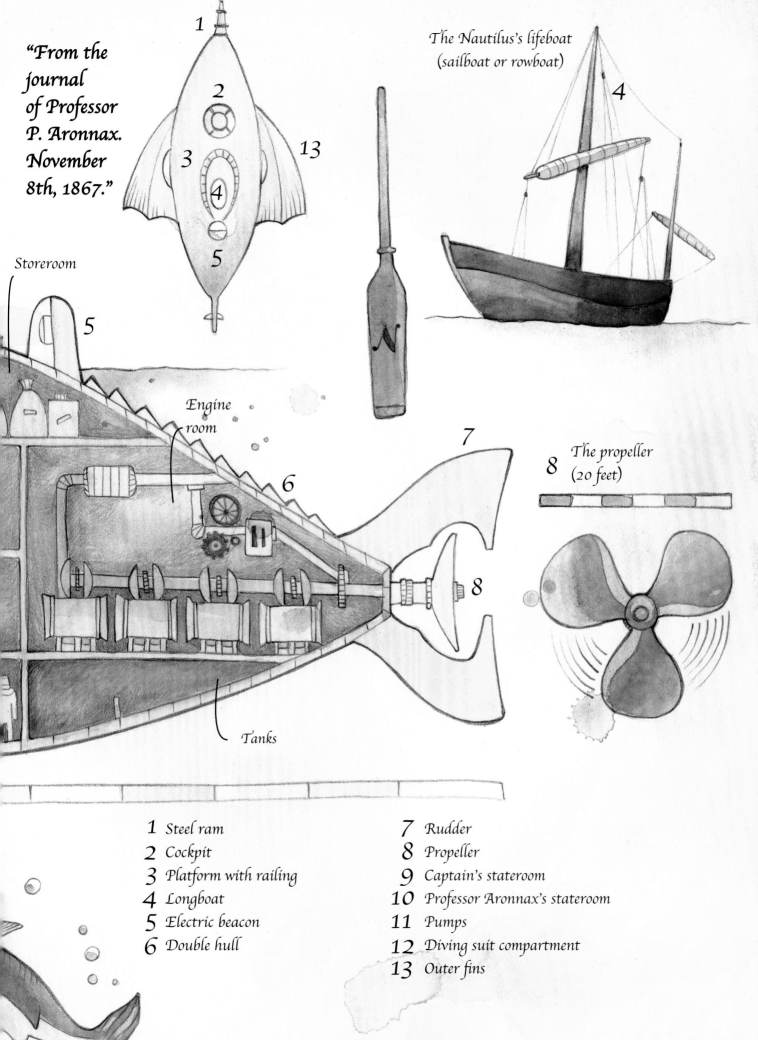

"From the journal of Professor P. Aronnax. November 8th, 1867."

1

2

3

13

4

5

Storeroom

5

The Nautilus's lifeboat (sailboat or rowboat)

4

Engine room

6

7

8

The propeller (20 feet)

8

Tanks

1 Steel ram
2 Cockpit
3 Platform with railing
4 Longboat
5 Electric beacon
6 Double hull

7 Rudder
8 Propeller
9 Captain's stateroom
10 Professor Aronnax's stateroom
11 Pumps
12 Diving suit compartment
13 Outer fins

After dinner, we all fell deeply asleep. I was the first to awaken,
but my companions woke up soon after.

I was the first to wake up from that deep sleep, but my companions
awakened soon after. Ned Land was hungrier than ever,
unsurprisingly – as, by my calculations, we had been asleep for nearly
a whole day. We remained isolated in our cell, our hunger growing,
along with Ned's rage, as the hours passed. We finally heard some
footsteps outside, and the door opened. No sooner had the door
opened than Ned rushed forward, but then we heard a voice speaking
in French.

"Calm down, Ned Land! And as to you, Professor – kindly listen
to me!"

It was the commander who had spoken.

"I didn't answer you yesterday because, after listening to your story,
I needed time to think things over and decide what to do.
A calamity has brought you into my presence."

"Unintentionally, if I may be so bold," I exclaimed.

The commander continued, raising his voice.

"Was it perhaps unintentionally that you hunted me on every sea and
fired your cannon at me? I am thus well within my rights to consider
you my enemies," he added, both anger and scorn in his voice now.

He fell silent for a long moment, then went on: "Since chance has brought you on board my vessel, however, on board you shall remain. In exchange for the freedom to observe everything that happens here, know this – it's possible that unforeseen events may force me to confine you to this cabin for a few hours, or even days, at a time."

"Pardon me, sir, but I don't call this freedom – this is a prison, it's sheer cruelty."

"You're wrong, Professor: it's an act of mercy. You attacked me and are now my prisoners of war! You have learned a secret that nobody in the world was ever meant to know. And instead of throwing you back into the depths of the ocean, I have decided to spare your lives."

"If this is the case, there is nothing more to add, save that we will not pledge to honor any promises."

"It is decided, then," the stranger said.

"One last question, sir – what are we to call you?"

"You may call me Captain Nemo. And you are now passengers on the *Nautilus*."

Then he turned to the steward, giving him orders in that strange language none of us recognized. The other man accompanied Ned and Conseil to their cabin, where a meal had been prepared for them. Thus they could finally leave the room where we had been held prisoners for several days.

"Your own dinner is also ready, Professor. Allow me to lead the way."

Walking down a lighted passageway, we came to a dining room
where a table had been laid for us.

Though I recognized many of the dishes, all fish-based, others
were completely unfamiliar to me.

"All these foods are healthy and nourishing, Professor.
Eat them without fear, although they may be new to you.
They are all products of the sea, as are the clothes you're
now wearing, woven from the fabric of certain shellfish.
The sea gives us everything and is everything to us!"

When we had finished our dinner, the captain invited me
on a tour of the *Nautilus*, so I rose to follow him.

A double door opened at the rear of the dining room, and
we entered what was undoubtedly a library.

Tall wooden bookcases were lined with uniformly-bound
volumes: books on science, philosophy and literature in every
language imaginable.

"I own 12,000 volumes – my only remaining ties with dry land,
which I was done with forever the day the *Nautilus* submerged
for the first time. These books are naturally at your disposal,
Professor – you may consult them freely."

Among these books, I recognized one which I knew had been published in 1865, thus concluding that the *Nautilus* couldn't have submerged before then. This meant that its underwater existence had begun no more than three years earlier.

As Captain Nemo opened another door, we entered an immense, well-lit lounge with high ceilings decorated in arabesques. It was an actual museum, filled with the wonders of the natural and artistic worlds.

"I used to love collecting works of art, and would travel to all the corners of the earth to seek them out."

Aside from many paintings adorning the walls and statues of classic antiquity mounted on their pedestals, the room held a stunning collection of natural rarities.

"I see you're admiring my shell collection, professor. They are, indeed, fascinating to a naturalist, but for me their charm goes way beyond their incredible shapes. I collected every one of them with my own two hands, searching every sea on the globe."

We then moved on the captain's stateroom, which adjoined my own. It was an austere room, yet many instruments were hanging on the walls.

"I'm unfamiliar with several of the instruments I see. Indeed, some of these devices are so strange-looking that I can't even hazard a guess as to their uses. May I ask you to satisfy my curiosity and tell me what they're for?"

Pleased by my obvious admiration and curiosity, Captain Nemo invited me to be seated, then began to speak. "These are all the instruments needed to navigate the *Nautilus*. Some are no doubt familiar to you – the thermometer to measure inside temperature and the barometer to measure outside pressure; the compass to steer my courses; the sextant, which tells me my latitude; chronometers to calculate my longitude and, finally, my spyglasses."

"What about this dial, and those strange probes?" I asked, dissatisfied with such cursory explanations.

"That dial is a pressure gauge to measure the depth at which we are navigating, while those are thermometric sounding lines that report the water temperatures in the different strata."

"I see. And what about the rest of your mechanical equipment, with all these bizarre parts?"

"All the instruments you see are powered by electricity – which

greatly differs from the electricity used by the rest of the world. Ours comes from the ocean, which generates it and allows us to live. But that's all I can tell you," my host added decisively. So we continued our tour of the *Nautilus*. A ladder in the middle of the submarine led to the upper end. "That goes to the longboat, which we use for fishing trips. A double opening allows you to pass directly into the launch," the captain explained. We then continued towards the lounge, where I was joined by Ned Land and Conseil. I told them all I had seen and, when I had finished, Ned asked if I knew anything of the crew. "I can't say, my dear Ned; that area is inaccessible, but you may as well give up any idea of taking over the *Nautilus*. This boat is an ingenious piece of work, so we should just wait and see what will happen."

"*Wait and see?!*" exploded Ned. "We're being held prisoner here, at sea with absolutely no idea what's on the other side... "

But before he could finish, we were suddenly plunged into darkness, and began to hear a strange sound. Then daylight flooded the lounge, and we realized there were just two glass panels separating us from the sea. Feeling like we were in an immense aquarium, we stared at the ocean depths in wonder.

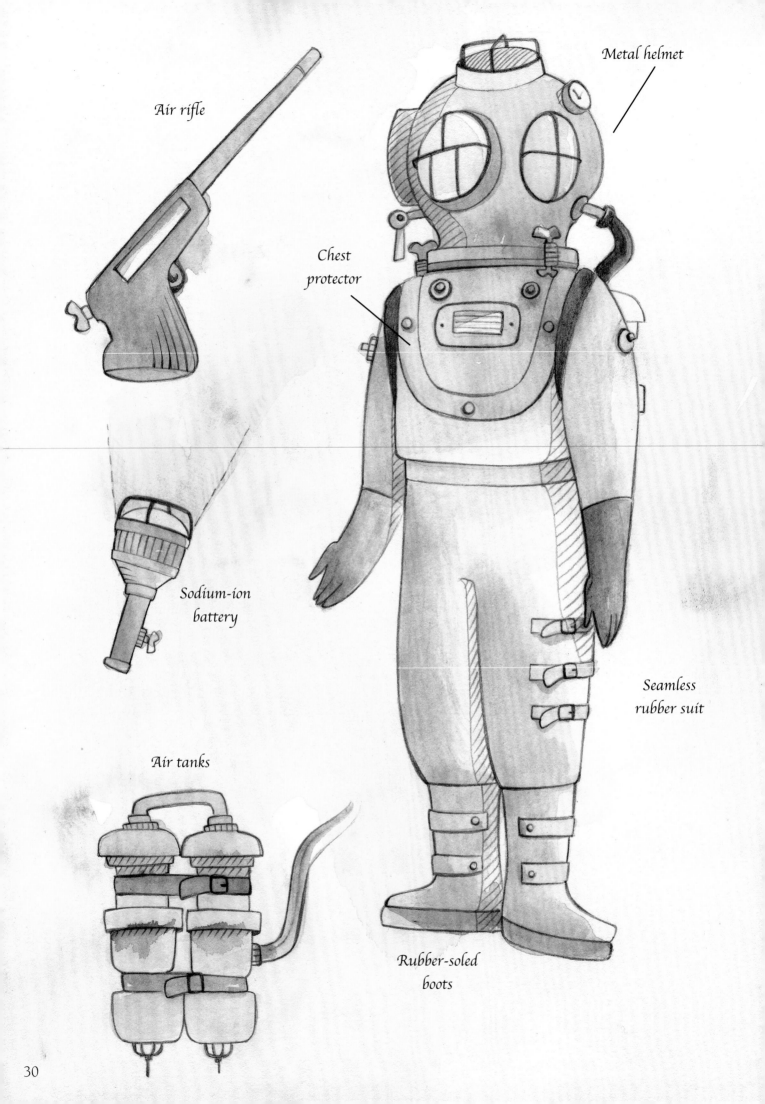

Air rifle

Metal helmet

Chest
protector

Sodium-ion
battery

Seamless
rubber suit

Air tanks

Rubber-soled
boots

From that moment on, I began keeping a journal of these adventures. Several days passed with no more visits from Captain Nemo, until one morning I found a note in my stateroom:
"Captain Nemo invites Professor Aronnax and his companions to join him on a hunting trip in the Crespo Island forests."
"A hunting trip!" exclaimed Ned.
"That means we'll be going ashore!" added Conseil.
"There's not a shadow of doubt – we must accept," Ned concluded.
I consulted a map, discovering that Crespo Island was a small rock in the middle of the Pacific Ocean.
I met Captain Nemo at breakfast time the next day. "Just out of curiosity, Captain… How can you explain this hunting trip, if you've truly severed all ties with the Earth?"
"Well, Professor, I forgot to mention that the Crespo Island forests are actually under water."
"Are you telling me that we're going hunting on the ocean floor?"
"Certainly! Without getting our feet wet and rifles in hand. Come, follow me."
Passing by Ned and Conseil's cabin, together we went on towards a sort of storeroom.
"You see, Professor – you'll be wearing a diving suit with a tank fastened on your back, containing the oxygen you need to breathe. This bizarre-looking lantern goes on your belt, and you'll use an air rifle to hunt with."
Ned decided not to join us on the expedition, but Conseil and I put on our diving suits and inserted our heads into the spherical headgear, feeling the air flow naturally. Thus equipped, we entered a cabin, the door closed behind us and we were surrounded by utter darkness.

sea, then crossing the seaweed forest of Crespo Island.

What an unforgettable experience! I found myself walking over plains of sand at the bottom of the

After a few minutes, my feet began to feel cold and, a few seconds later, I found myself treading the sandy seabed. I was soon able to make out some shapes in the distance – rocks covered in zoophyte specimens and shells, mollusks and polyps… What an amazing sight! After a while, the seabed became carpeted in algae, and Captain Nemo pointed to a dark mass ahead of us: the forest of Crespo Island. This forest was made up of treelike plants, and as we passed beneath their arches, I was struck by the bizarre arrangement of their branches. All the plants and tree branches rose towards the surface of the ocean, as if the forest were growing upwards. Different types of trees towered above flowering shrubs that were also covered in zoophytes. We continued our hike, the plants dwindling as we descended to greater depths. After walking for several hours, we came to an insurmountable wall of rocks – the foundations of Crespo Island. It was time to return to the *Nautilus*, albeit following a different path. Light reappeared as we climbed upwards, and we found ourselves walking amid a swarm of fish when we spied a sea otter moving through the bushes. It was a magnificent animal, with its brown and silver fur coat, comical round head and whiskers like a cat's.

We were still walking when Captain Nemo and his seaman suddenly threw Conseil and me to the ground. When I raised my head, I saw two enormous shadows passing swiftly over us: a couple of sharks! Luckily, they didn't see us. We reached the *Nautilus* half an hour later, reentering through its double doors. Conseil and I removed our diving suits and went back to our cabins, exhausted yet still amazed by our incredible excursion on the bottom of the sea.

Several days later, I found myself on the platform with Captain Nemo, scanning the horizon. I could see several islets of unequal size, surrounded by a coral reef.

"You see the islands of Vanikoro ahead of us?" said Captain Nemo.

"The famous islands that countless vessels have crashed against?"

"The very ones, Professor."

Meanwhile, the *Nautilus* continued on its journey and, after crossing the treacherous waters of the Coral Sea off the northern coast of Australia, we finally sighted the coast of Papua. Captain Nemo expressed a desire to reach the Indian Ocean via the perilous Torres Strait – strewn with rocks, reefs and islets, navigation here is a dangerous and difficult activity.

He thus took every possible precaution in crossing it. We moved at a moderate pace and, though the sea was rough, the *Nautilus* managed to slip through the towering reefs, heading towards Gueboroa Island, where it unfortunately ran aground among the rocks made even more dangerous at low tide.

Observing the captain speak with his second-in-command, I approached them to ask what was going on.

"Just a slight accident, Professor. We have run aground, but luckily the tide will turn in a few days, and the *Nautilus* can resume its journey."

As soon as I shared this news with my companions, Ned Land exclaimed: "Why can't we get the lay of the land, as long as we're here? Explore the island, hunt some wild game for a change?"

"I agree with Ned. Couldn't Master persuade his friend, Captain Nemo, to allow us to explore the island?" added Conseil.

Though I was hesitant to ask, and much to my surprise, Captain Nemo granted us permission to go ashore. We found the longboat ready for us the very next morning.

Armed with electric rifles and axes, we slowly left the *Nautilus* behind and made for dry land.

"Land!" Ned kept repeating happily. After so many months at sea, he couldn't wait to set foot on familiar soil. So we took up our oars, eager to explore the forests and hunt all the delicious meat hidden within.

When we finally reached dry land, we were impressed by our surroundings. We trod the ground carefully, advancing with great caution.

Tall trees of every kind towered above us, and Ned suddenly rushed towards one, which he recognized as a coconut tree, to pick some of its fruits.

As we moved on, we discovered several types of edible fruit, most of which Ned Land was familiar with from his past trips. We went deeper and deeper into the forest until, realizing we were laden with sufficient provisions, we decided to go back to the *Nautilus*.

The next morning, we found the longboat ready for us, so we set off once again for the island, hoping for a more successful hunting expedition.

That day, we decided to explore the other side of the island. Coasting along stream after stream, we reached a high clearing surrounded by trees.

A large number of birds of different breeds were soaring above the water, but we were unable to draw near, as they were clearly used to the presence of man.

After crossing a meadow, we found ourselves in a small wood where a host of parrots were flying from tree to tree; we then entered a dense thicket, where other magnificent birds soared into the air as they heard us rustling through the bushes.

"Birds of paradise!" I cried.

They were superb examples of the birds that inhabit those lands, their long plumage arranged so as to cause them to head into the wind.

Capturing one of them, and the chance to study these spectacular birds from up close, would have been a dream come true for me.

After an hour's walk, Conseil, who was in the lead, bent down with a triumphant shout. He had found a bird of paradise, lying motionless under a tree. The poor beast could barely move its head; it looked drunk, and perhaps it was, from the nutmeg it had been devouring. Whatever the reason, its helplessness was a stroke of luck for us, as it allowed us to examine it at our leisure. By observing its uniquely-shaped tail feathers, I was able to identify it as a "great emerald", one of the rarest specimens of the species.

The bird measured about twelve inches long, and had a small head, with eyes set near the juncture of the beak.

Its multi-hued plumage was breathtakingly beautiful: what a stunning bird! Suddenly aware of our presence, the bird managed to rouse itself and began to chirp indignantly – no doubt due to our prolonged scrutiny. As it was still unable to fly, however, capturing it presented no difficulty. So we set off again, happy to have found a bird of paradise, at least, when Ned finally managed to bring down a wild boar and some specimens of "rabbit kangaroos".

Pleased with the results of our hunting expedition, we went back to the beach, where we prepared an excellent meat dinner. We were sitting around, talking and eating, when a stone suddenly landed at our feet.

Bird of Paradise
New Guinea.
Up to 16 inches

Mainly
frugivorous
diet

♂

♀

Paradisaea apoda

(Bird of Paradise)

Male specimen portrayed
during mating ritual

We jumped to our feet, only to see a horde of savages
storming towards us, armed with bows and arrows.
"Head for the longboat!" I shouted.
Loading our provisions into the longboat, we pushed it into
the sea and began rowing with all our might.
Howling and gesticulating, the savages followed us into the
sea. We reached the *Nautilus* in less than twenty minutes and
hurried aboard, immediately warning the captain about the
savages who had chased us into the sea.
Shaken and frightened as we were by the encounter, Captain
Nemo seemed to have no fears, and thus reassured, we retired
to our cabins.

Climbing onto the platform early the next morning, I saw that the islanders had reached the coral reef, taking advantage of the low tide. They were close enough that I could make their features out clearly: athletic in build, they had large noses and long, wild hair gathered up with leaves of grass and feathers. They were practically naked, men and women alike wearing only grass skirts made of banana leaves. They wore beaded necklaces around their necks, and were all armed with bows, arrows and daggers. When the tide began to rise, however, the islanders retreated towards the beach. It seemed like we were out of danger… but several hours later, we discovered that some twenty dugout canoes had surrounded the *Nautilus*.

bows and arrows – didn't even come close to scratching its double hull.

The Nautilus was surrounded and attacked by a local tribe, but the warriors – though armed with

Hollowed out of tree trunks, these dugouts were steered by skillful, half-naked – as far as I could see – oarsmen. As soon as they were close enough, they hurled a shower of arrows at the *Nautilus*.

"Captain, the natives have surrounded us in their dugouts!" I announced anxiously.

"Thank you, Professor Aronnax. We shall close the hatches immediately."

"All right, sir, but what about tomorrow, when we'll need to reopen the hatches to change the *Nautilus*'s air? How will we keep the islanders from climbing aboard?"

"Oh, Professor… Have faith, and you shall see," said Captain Nemo, as he retired to his stateroom.

I slept poorly that night, hearing the islanders walking on the platform and yelling to one another.

The next morning, the hatches had not yet been opened, and I tried to take my mind off things by devoting myself to my studies.

Early in the afternoon, I felt the *Nautilus* moving, raised by the tide, and the captain entered the lounge to announce our imminent departure.

"I've also given orders to open the hatches," he told me.

"But won't the islanders try to enter?"

"Follow me, Professor, and we shall see."

So we headed for the main companionway, where we found Ned Land and Conseil, who were as puzzled as I was.

The first islander to set foot on the ramp was thrown backwards, and the same went for his companion. I then realized that the ramp was charged with electricity; anyone who touched it received a terrible – though not deadly – shock. As the natives gave up and retreated towards their forest, the *Nautilus*, lifted by the tide, was finally able to depart, leaving behind the perilous waters of the Torres Strait.

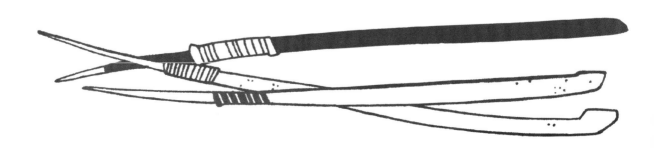

All went smoothly for several days. One morning, however, I climbed onto the platform to find Captain Nemo scanning the horizon through his spyglass, which he then lowered to speak to his second-in-command. The captain strolled restlessly from one end of the platform to the other, stopping every now and then to look out to sea. His second-in-command also kept lifting his spyglass to examine the horizon. Puzzled by these actions, I went below to my stateroom to get my own spyglass, in the hopes of discovering what lay ahead of us. But no sooner had I raised it to my eyes than Captain Nemo signaled for me to put it down.

"I'm sorry, Professor, but I must ask you to honor the agreement we made. I must briefly confine you and your companions to the cabin where you spent your early days on board the *Nautilus*."

So I went below to inform Ned Land and Conseil of what I had been told. We were taken to our cell in no time, and lunch was served soon afterwards. As we ate, we continued to wonder what could be happening on board the *Nautilus* without, however, coming up with any logical hypotheses. As soon as we were done with our meal, the lights in the room went out, leaving us in the dark. To my astonishment, Ned Land soon fell asleep, as did Conseil. Strangely enough, I soon became sleepy too. I tried to keep my eyes open, but couldn't.

Our food had obviously been laced with sleep-inducing substances to keep us from finding out what was happening.

No sooner had I heard the hatches close – apparently, the *Nautilus* was preparing to submerge once more – than I fell into a deep slumber.

When I woke up the next morning, I found myself in my stateroom. Someone had obviously taken us back to our own lodgings, which meant we were free again. I hurried up to the platform, where I found Ned Land and Conseil waiting for me. All seemed normal, as if nothing unusual had happened on board the *Nautilus*. There was no sign of Captain Nemo that morning, but he joined me later in the lounge, making no mention of the events of the previous evening but simply asking: "Are you a doctor, Professor Aronnax?"

"Yes, Captain."

"Then would you come with me? I need you to see to one of my men."

It was, of course, the captain himself who led me to the sick man. Unfortunately, as I bent over him, I realized he was gravely wounded as well as sick. From the looks of the man's head wound, it was clear he didn't have much longer to live.

The captain explained how the *Nautilus* had suffered a collision that cracked one of the engine levers, which in turn had struck the poor seaman on the head.

Tears ran silently down Nemo's face and, deeply moved by what I had seen, I withdrew to my stateroom, leaving him with the dying man. The next morning, Captain Nemo was already on deck when I arrived. He came over as soon as he saw me and invited me, along with my companions, to join him on another underwater expedition, that very day.

I rejoined Ned and Conseil to inform them of Captain Nemo's proposal; this time they both accepted, and we hurried to the cabin to put on our diving suits.

Carpeted in coral instead of sand, the sea bottom was completely different compared to the Pacific Ocean. During our journey, we came across a series of tangled bushes, the light producing indescribably beautiful effects as we passed. After about two hours of walking deeper and deeper under the sea, Captain Nemo and his men halted in the center of a clearing surrounded by trees. Four of them were carrying a strange object, and my companions and I looked on, trying to understand what was happening.

When one of the men began digging a hole, it dawned on me that they had come to bury their dead companion in a coral cemetery.

When the grave was finally deep enough, they lowered the body into it, then Captain Nemo and his men knelt to bid a final farewell to their friend.

Afterwards, we all turned back towards the *Nautilus*, deeply moved by the experience we had shared.

Argonaut

These graceful animals swim backwards. They have six slender tentacles for swimming, and two palm-shaped ones which spread upward like sails.

Several peaceful days followed, as we sailed the waters of the Indian Ocean at a depth between four and seven hundred feet, admiring the incredible underwater marvels when the metal plates were removed from the glass panels.

Though the days on board the *Nautilus* were all much the same, and may have seemed long and monotonous, I myself was never bored. My pleasant strolls along the platform when we would surface, the depths of the sea I never tired of admiring from the windows, the endless books to be read in the library and the writing of my journal, where I recorded all my experiences – all this kept me busy and happy. Furthermore, we enjoyed good health, the cuisine on board was excellent, and every day brought something new and incredible. After cruising along Keeling Island, the *Nautilus* set its course towards the tip of the Indian peninsula, where the rough waters caused it to slow down.

Once, when the *Nautilus* was on the surface, Conseil and I happened to be on the platform in time to witness a marvelous sight.

There is an unusual animal, even among the countless sea creatures, which is said to bring good luck to anyone who

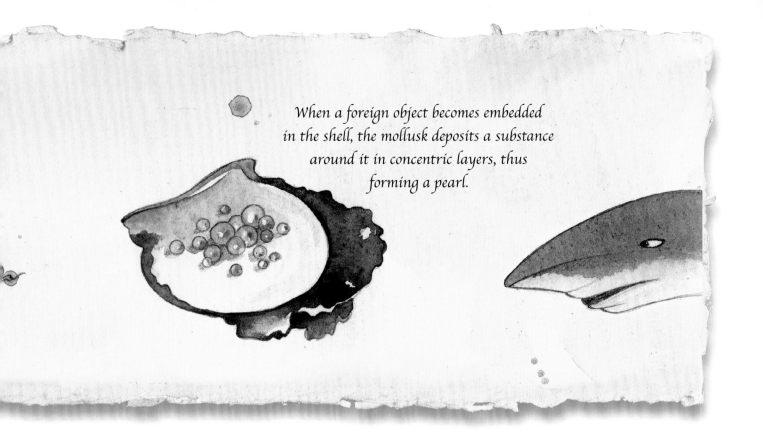

When a foreign object becomes embedded
in the shell, the mollusk deposits a substance
around it in concentric layers, thus
forming a pearl.

happens to see it. The ancients – Aristotle, Athenaeus, Pliny –
called it *Nautilus Pompylius*, but it is now known by the name of
"argonaut".

And now, while Conseil and I were enjoying a spectacular
sunset, we saw a school of argonauts floating on the surface of
the ocean.

There were too many of them to count, but I believe we saw at
least a hundred. I recognized them as tuberculate argonauts, a
species exclusive to the seas near India. These peculiar mollusks
were swimming backwards by means of their locomotive tubes,
breathing in water and then expelling it. Part of their bodies
was hidden under a sort of shell. Six of their eight tentacles, the
longer ones, were floating on the surface of the water, while the
other two were rounded into palms, spreading upwards like
sails. We could clearly make out the undulating, spiral-shaped
shells that transport the animals without sticking to them.

"You see, Conseil, the argonaut could break away from its home
if it chose to. It is free to leave its shell, yet never does so."

"Not unlike Captain Nemo," Conseil replied wisely. "He is
similar to the argonauts, as he could leave the *Nautilus* at any
time – even just to take a walk on dry land. Yet he never does."

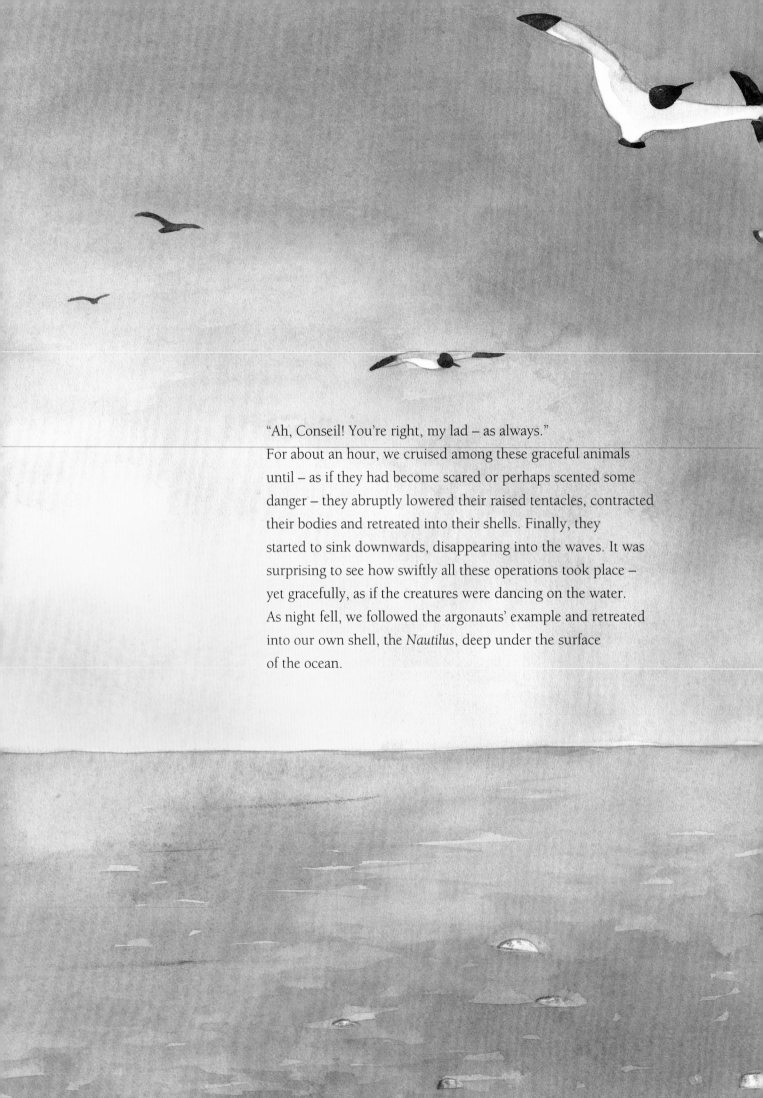

"Ah, Conseil! You're right, my lad – as always."

For about an hour, we cruised among these graceful animals
until – as if they had become scared or perhaps scented some
danger – they abruptly lowered their raised tentacles, contracted
their bodies and retreated into their shells. Finally, they
started to sink downwards, disappearing into the waves. It was
surprising to see how swiftly all these operations took place –
yet gracefully, as if the creatures were dancing on the water.
As night fell, we followed the argonauts' example and retreated
into our own shell, the *Nautilus*, deep under the surface
of the ocean.

When the *Nautilus* finally resurfaced, I could see some mountains and other bizarrely-shaped outlines, so I hurried down to the lounge to check our position on the chart. My assessments showed us to be just off the island of Ceylon. Captain Nemo appeared just then and, glancing at the chart, turned towards me and said: "This island is famous for its pearls, Professor Aronnax. Would you and your companions like to visit a pearl fishery? We won't see any fishermen because the harvest usually begins in March. The waters fill with fishermen diving into the sea with a stone attached to their boats by a rope, to help them reach greater depths. It's late January now, so I doubt we'll come across any... But you never know; some may have set to work early."

"I'm sure the pearl fishery will be fascinating even without any fisherman, Captain! We'll go with you with great pleasure."

"By the way, Professor Aronnax, are you afraid of sharks? Who knows, we might come across some tomorrow… In which case, you'll also have the chance to witness a shark hunt!" Later, when I met Ned Land and Conseil, I found them eager to join the new expedition, which the captain had already told them about. Judging from their carefree expressions, however, he hadn't mentioned the sharks. "What exactly is a pearl, sir?" asked Ned curiously.

"My dear Ned, a pearl is something ever-changing in the eyes of the beholder. For the ladies, it's a beautiful jewel; for us naturalists, on the other hand, it's simply a secretion produced in a sort of shell by a valuable mollusk, the pearl oyster."

We were awakened early the next morning. Climbing into the longboat, we headed for the coasts of Mannar Island. Once we reached the bay where the fishermen would soon gather to go fishing, we plunged into the water.

Surrounded, as usual, by a breathtaking array of fish and bright colors,

we finally arrived at the place where the pearl oysters reproduce.
Most of the countless mollusks clinging to the rocks would
soon be harvested by the fishermen, but millions more of the
creatures would appear in the same place within a year.
Captain Nemo moved on, leading us to a cave hollowed out
of the rocks. We followed him in, sure that the captain had
some mysterious secret to share with us. Sure enough, after
going down a steep slope, we came to a small circular clearing,
where Nemo signaled to us to stop. That's when we saw an
enormous oyster ahead of us; it was over three feet long!
The captain had brought us there to show it to us, but I assume
that he also wished to check on its condition. Approaching
the oyster, he forced it open with his dagger to see how much
the pearl inside had grown.
It was a pearl of astounding size, almost as big as a coconut!
Too large to wear, of course, but undoubtedly a jewel
of incalculable value, which would someday – when
the time was right – make its way into Captain Nemo's
personal museum. We left the cave after this visit, and
were heading back to the *Nautilus* when Captain Nemo
came to a sudden halt.
Terrified that the captain had spied a shark, I soon realized –
to my great relief – that I was wrong.
He pointed to a dark shadow dropping to the seafloor – a
fisherman who had started his harvest a few months ahead
of time. We could see the shadow of his boat above. The man
would grip a stone as he dove, then ascend by means of a rope
connecting the stone to his boat.
Though he went up and down several times, he was unable
to gather many oysters, as he had to tear them from the banks
where they were clinging tightly.
We were observing the diver's careful movements when all of
a sudden, as he knelt on the seafloor, he became frightened.
Speechless with panic, we watched him trying to reach the
surface, threatened by a gigantic shadow.

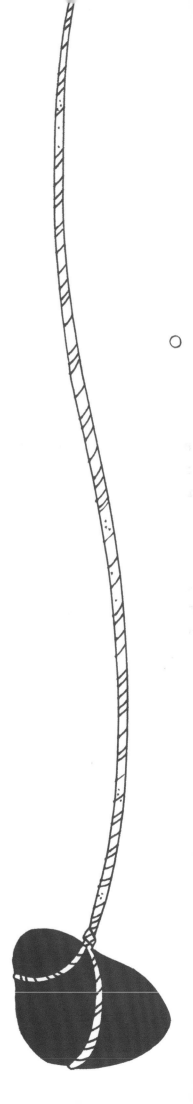

shark. Thank goodness Captain Nemo was able to save him!

I'll never forget the terror I felt when I saw the pearl fisherman being chased by an enormous

It was the shadow of an enormous shark. The animal hurled itself at the fisherman, who avoided its sharp jaws by jumping to the side, but couldn't escape the trashing of its tail, which threw him to the ground.

As the shark swam back to sink its teeth into its prey, Captain Nemo rushed to the diver's aid. When the shark saw the captain, it headed swiftly towards him. Captain Nemo stood motionless and composed and, when the shark was within reach, managed to leap aside and thrust his dagger into its belly. The sea was dyed red, but the battle had just begun.

Through the water, opaque from the blood pouring from the animal's wound, I could barely make out an enormous dark mass thrashing about, while the captain clung to one of the shark's fins, attempting to stab it once more with his dagger.

As it struggled, the shark managed to knock the captain to the seafloor. Just then, Ned Land launched his harpoon in the timeliest of fashions, driving it straight into the shark's heart to deal the finishing blow.

We rushed towards Captain Nemo as he stood up, fortunately uninjured. Going over to the fisherman, the captain cut the rope binding him to his stone and together we rose to the surface. I feared for the poor man, who had spent a long time under water without breathing, but Conseil and the captain massaged him until he regained consciousness. How the sight of us standing over him, in our bizarre suits and headgear, must have frightened him!

Captain Nemo pulled out a small bag of pearls and placed it, as a gift, in the man's still-trembling hands.

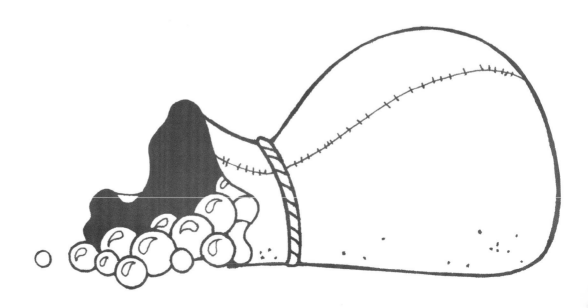

Taking our leave of the fisherman, we began to retrace our steps, and within half an hour had reached the longboat that would take us back to the *Nautilus*.

Once we had left the island of Ceylon behind us, Ned Land asked me where we were going.

"Our course shows us heading towards the Gulf of Oman, between Arabia and the Indian Peninsula, then towards the Persian Gulf and perhaps even towards the Red Sea, who knows!"

"But, Professor… the Persian Gulf and the Red Sea are both landlocked, since the Suez Canal is just a strip of land that hasn't been cut all the way through yet! Once we enter, we'll have to turn back."

"We'll see, my dear Ned, where the captain takes us!"

As the *Nautilus* cruised along the Gulf of Oman, we recognized Muscat, one of its most famous towns. Then the submarine sank fathoms below, and a few days later we finally found ourselves surrounded by the waters of the Red Sea. Through the glass panels, I observed the crystal-clear water dotted with countless brilliantly-colored fish and magnificent sponges of all shapes and sizes. "Well, Professor, what do you think of the Red Sea with all its hidden wonders?" "Well, Captain," I replied. "Admiring its depths has been a great joy. Yet I am curious as to how it got its name. The waters we have cruised through are anything but red…"

"That's because we're still too far from the gulf. You'll see the color change as we ascend… We can't cross the Suez Canal, but you'll be able to admire the breathtaking landscape of Port Said, which will take us into the Mediterranean." I soon discovered how this

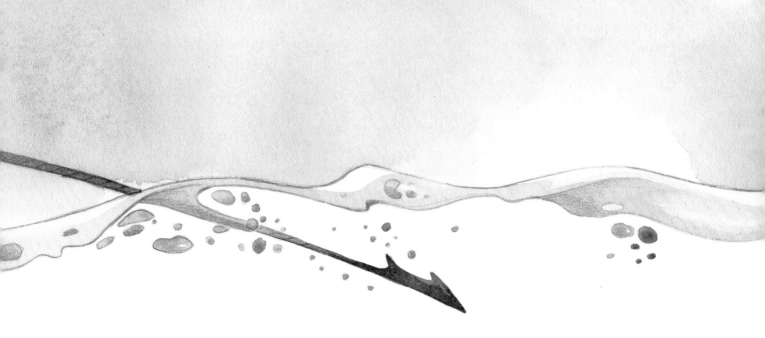

could be. Captain Nemo knew of an underwater passageway, which he had named the "Arabic Tunnel". He was doubtless the only man on Earth to have ever crossed it. The next day, when I was on the platform with Ned and Conseil, Ned pointed to a mass out in the middle of the sea: "Do you see anything? What kind of animal could that be? It's not a whale, is it?"
"It's a dugong!" I replied. "There are very few specimens of this peculiar creature in the Red Sea." Ned kept staring at it, his eyes ablaze. He was a harpooner, after all, and would have given anything to have his weapon in hand to attack the creature. Just then, we were joined by Captain Nemo. Understanding Ned's frame of mind, he ordered the longboat to be prepared for us, so we could hunt our prey, which would also make an excellent meal. The closer we got to the sea creature, the better we could see it: it had an elongated body ending in long, tapering flukes, two shorter lateral fins and sharp teeth. Ned hurled his harpoon, hitting the animal which, however, soon resurfaced and attacked our boat. After several attempts, Ned was finally able to pierce it through the heart and, hoisting our haul onto the longboat, we returned to the *Nautilus*. We then set off again, soon finding ourselves near the Suez Canal. A few days later, the captain informed me that we were about to reach the famous tunnel. He told me, furthermore, that the passageway was especially treacherous, so he would direct maneuvers himself, and invited me to join him in the pilothouse.

When the fateful day came, I followed the captain towards the central companionway, which led to the upper gangways and then to the pilothouse, which stood at one end of the platform.

The wheel stood in the center of the cabin, and all four walls were made of glass, so we could see in every direction. Though the cabin was dark, the sea all around us was lit up by the *Nautilus*'s lights. This cabin was linked to the engine room by means of electric wires, so the captain could send orders to his men and signal the direction he wished us to take by pressing a button.

"And now, Professor, it's time to look for that tunnel."

With my hands up against the glass, I couldn't take my eyes off the rocky formations that were unfolding before me, so close that I could see the magnificent zoophytes, corals, algae and crustaceans covering them.

We followed this barrier for about an hour, during which Captain Nemo never took his eyes off the compass.

"Do you see the tunnel ahead of us, Professor?" he asked at a certain point, as he took the helm himself.

The *Nautilus* slipped into the deep, dark tunnel, and Captain Nemo left the steering wheel twenty minutes later.

"Here we are, Professor… the Mediterranean."

The *Nautilus* resurfaced at dawn the next morning, and I hurried up to the platform, where Ned and Conseil soon joined me.

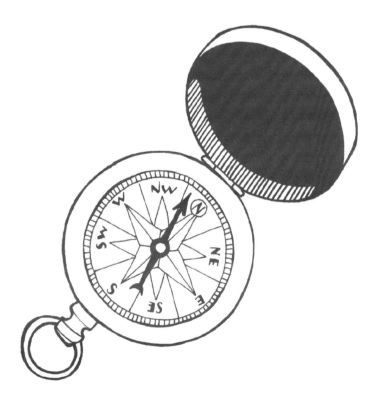

The pilothouse is amazing! It has four glass walls, so you can see in every direction and admire the wonders of the sea bottom.

"As you can see, my friends, we've reached the Mediterranean."

"Good!" Ned exclaimed. "Once we get close enough to the coast, we can make our escape by night, in the longboat."

Poor Ned, as restless as ever, was itching to escape the *Nautilus*. And he had a point: we were back in well-connected territories, although a part of me wished to remain on board and continue exploring the great ocean depths with Captain Nemo.

"Fine, Ned. If an opportunity arises, just alert us, and we'll follow you," I said.

In the next few days, however, the *Nautilus* hardly ever rose to the surface. Perhaps, seeing how heavily traveled the sea was, the captain wished to escape notice. As I observed the charts, I realized

we were cruising towards Crete although, for reasons unknown to me, the glass panels remained sealed. I remembered how, at the time we had boarded the *Abraham Lincoln*, the island was in rebellion against the Turkish rule. But who knew what had happened afterwards? One evening, I happened to be alone in the lounge with Captain Nemo, who was silent and preoccupied. He ordered that the panels be lifted, and I saw him examining the seafloor with great care, as if he were searching for something. Meanwhile, I was studying the magnificent specimens of fish that passed before my eyes when a man suddenly appeared out of nowhere, wearing a leather bag at his belt. The man swam towards us, sometimes rising to the surface to breathe, then diving back underwater. As he drew nearer, he finally pressed his face against the glass of the *Nautilus* to stare at us. I yelled in surprised, and was even more surprised to see Captain Nemo signal to the man. "Have no fear, Professor; this man lives more in the sea than on shore. He's nicknamed *The Fish*, and is well-known all over the Cyclades for his bold diving exploits. He swims from island to island, even going as far as Crete."

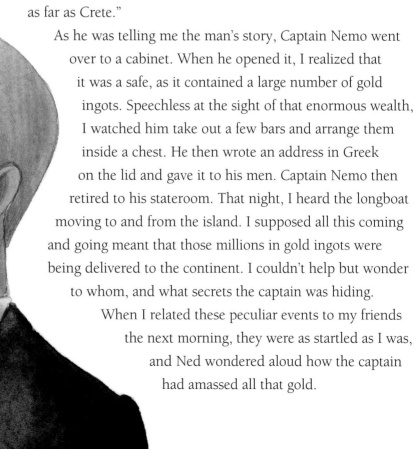

As he was telling me the man's story, Captain Nemo went over to a cabinet. When he opened it, I realized that it was a safe, as it contained a large number of gold ingots. Speechless at the sight of that enormous wealth, I watched him take out a few bars and arrange them inside a chest. He then wrote an address in Greek on the lid and gave it to his men. Captain Nemo then retired to his stateroom. That night, I heard the longboat moving to and from the island. I supposed all this coming and going meant that those millions in gold ingots were being delivered to the continent. I couldn't help but wonder to whom, and what secrets the captain was hiding.

When I related these peculiar events to my friends the next morning, they were as startled as I was, and Ned wondered aloud how the captain had amassed all that gold.

Meanwhile, leaving the Greek Islands behind, the *Nautilus* continued to plow the waves of the Mediterranean, the ideal blue sea. A historic sea, traveled since ancient times by Carthaginians, Greeks and Romans. In spite of its beauty, however, it seemed like this sea gave Captain Nemo no pleasure, judging by the *Nautilus*'s speed. In fact, Ned Land had to give up his escape plans, at least for the moment. Furthermore, the submarine rose to the surface only at night, to renew our air supply, and took care to stay away from the coasts.

These conditions were detrimental to my studies, as well; at this speed, it was hard to recognize and classify the marine life surrounding us. I did manage to view some Mediterranean fish, but barely caught a glimpse of many others.

By then, having rounded Libya, the *Nautilus* descended to even greater depths, and new and thrilling scenery appeared before my eyes. Countless vessels have perished in this part of the Mediterranean – from the Coast of Algiers to the beaches of Provence – over the years.

Though the Mediterranean is a semi-closed basin, its waters are far from calm; its often rough waves and unpredictable winds are enough to destroy the sturdiest of ships. And though we cruised

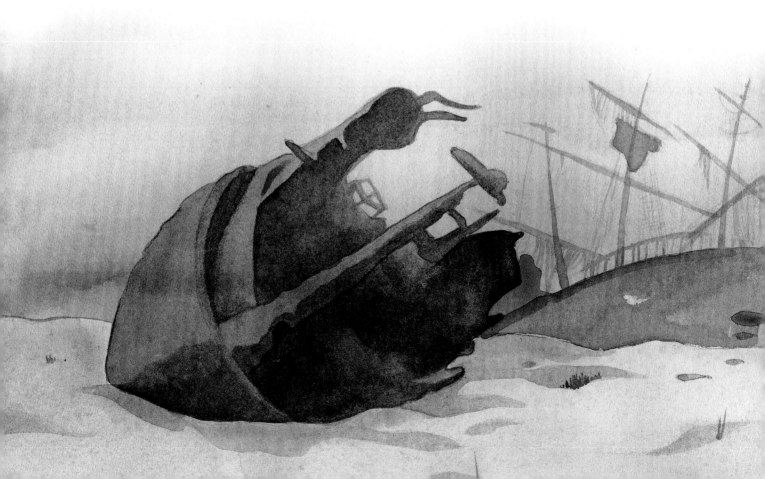

by swiftly, I could see with my own eyes how many vessels had
been swallowed up by this cruel sea. During our crossing of the
Mediterranean depths, the seafloor was strewn with wrecked
ships. The older wrecks were already encrusted with coral, while
the more recent ones were covered only by a layer of rust. I saw
anchors, cannons, shattered masts, tanks, iron timbers, engine
parts and pieces of wood everywhere. Some of these wrecked
ships had perished in collisions, while others had probably hit
some reefs. A few, with their masts still upright, had undoubtedly
sunk straight down.

It was a ghostly landscape, we realized as the *Nautilus* passed
by, shining its electric light among the wreckage.

The wrecks began to increase as we drew nearer to the Strait
of Gibraltar; collisions were more common in the narrow space
between the shores of Africa and Europe.

How many tragedies had unfolded in these Mediterranean
depths! Seeing them up close came as a great shock to me.

The *Nautilus*, meanwhile, took full advantage of the current flowing
into the ocean from the Mediterranean to cross the Strait of Gibraltar.
And in just a few hours, after barely two days cruising the
Mediterranean, we emerged into the waters of the Atlantic Ocean.

The *Nautilus* resurfaced as soon as we had emerged from the strait. Later, when I ran into Ned, he looked at me intently and said: "The time has finally come, Professor. We'll do it this evening. We're a few miles off the coast of Portugal, and it's too good a chance to miss. The longboat is ready, so Conseil and I will go to the central companionway at nine o'clock this evening; you'll stay in the library and wait for my signal."

I could make no objection, since who knew how long these ideal circumstances might last?

I spent the rest of the day in my stateroom, torn between a desire to regain my freedom and a desire to stay on board the *Nautilus* and continue exploring the marvels of the underwater world.

That day, I tried to avoid the captain, afraid that he might read my sadness at having to abandon the *Nautilus* in my eyes.

As I went to the lounge around seven in the evening, I passed by the captain's stateroom and, unable to help myself, took a few steps inside. I was immediately struck by some etchings I hadn't noticed on my first visit: portraits of the great men of history who had sacrificed their lives to an ideal.

I recognized Kosciusko, who fought for Polish independence; Lincoln, who abolished slavery and Washington, founder of the American Union.

I had just made my way to the library to wait for Ned Land's signal when the propellers suddenly shut off, and I wondered why. What was happening? Had our escape plans been discovered?

Captain Nemo entered while I was still lost in thought.

"Professor, if you're amenable, I'd like to tell you a curious tale."

And the captain began telling me about an event that took place in 1702.

"The Spanish territories were ruled by the French at the time, but Spain had been granted that its galleons, laden with gold from the Americas, could enter the port of Cadiz. Now, Spain was expecting a rich convoy in late 1702, but as the English fleet was also traveling those waters, the Spaniards decided to make for the Bay of Vigo, an open mooring that's almost impossible to defend. Sure enough, several English vessels soon arrived, and when the French admiral realized that all his wealth was about to fall into enemy hands, he set fire to the galleons, which sank to the bottom of the sea with their immense treasure. Well, Professor, we are actually in the Bay of Vigo now."

The captain gave orders for the panels to be opened, and looking through the glass I could see crewmen dressed in diving suits gathering gold ingots and gorgeous jewels on the bottom of the ocean. This, then, was how Captain Nemo amassed his great wealth, and this was why the propellers had been shut off and the *Nautilus* had abandoned the surface for the ocean floor.

The next morning, when I met Ned Land on the platform, he couldn't hide his disappointment. After all, the *Nautilus* had submerged just as we were about to escape. I went back to my studies, much more relaxed than the day before, and received a visit from Captain Nemo in the evening.

"Professor Aronnax, would you like to visit the ocean depths by night, even though it'll be a long, tiring walk?"

"With pleasure, Captain!"

The waters were pitch-black, but Captain Nemo pointed to a reddish spot in the distance that was giving off a sort of glow. Our path was getting steeper, as if we were climbing a mountain, and ever brighter, as we walked towards the reddish glow.

The captain set a brisk pace, and I followed. We came to a vast plateau where I observed gigantic stacks of stones, perhaps the ruins of ancient castles and temples. Continuing on our path, we finally came to the topmost peak. Opposite us, I spied another mountain – a volcano spewing torrents of lava, the source of the reddish glow we were following. An entire town in ruins spread out below me; its temples pulled down, its arches broken. The ruins of an acropolis. Where were we? As I looked around for Captain Nemo, I saw him coming towards me. Picking up a stone, he wrote a single word on a rock: "Atlantis".

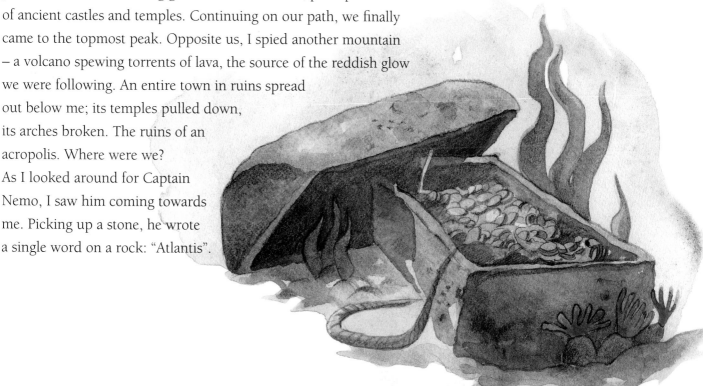

The next day, I described our nocturnal excursion to Conseil, who could still catch a glimpse of the submerged continent through the open panels as the *Nautilus* moved away. The ground grew rockier and covered in lava as we left the area, and a few hours later I noticed a sort of high wall blocking the horizon so we couldn't get by.

As its summit obviously rose above sea level, I supposed it to be a continent, or at the very least a large island, but I had no idea what our position was at the moment.

The panels were closed at nightfall, so I could no longer see anything, which was a pity. The *Nautilus* had reached the wall by now, and I would have liked to see how it got around it.

When I hurried up to the platform early the next morning, I was astonished to find myself surrounded by darkness. Had I made a mistake? Was it still nighttime? Yet not a single star was twinkling in the sky…

"Is that you, Professor?" came Captain Nemo's voice.

"Where are we?" I asked quickly.

"Underground."

"Underground? How can that be, if the *Nautilus* is still floating?"

The captain lit a beacon, and I could finally see our surroundings. We were floating on a sort of circular lake, and above us I spied an opening through which a faint light filtered. Were we in a cavern?

"Where are we?" I asked the captain again.

"We're inside an extinct volcano, Professor Aronnax. The *Nautilus* entered through a natural channel during the night."

"So the opening I see above is nothing but its crater?"

"Precisely," said the captain.

"And why are we here?"

"You see, Professor, the *Nautilus* runs on electricity produced entirely by elements taken from marine waters rather than the rocky bottoms. I extract sodium from the water, which of course is rich in salt. By mixing the sodium with other elements such as magnesium, I obtain an electric battery that is much more powerful than the average ones. To extract the sodium, I need the heat from carbon fuel, and this spot offers me inexhaustible coal mines. When we burn this combustible to produce sodium, the smoke escapes from the mountain's crater, giving it the appearance of a still-active volcano."

The captain explained that we would only stay there a day, and suggested we take advantage of the fact to explore the caverns and lagoon of the ancient volcano. So, along with Ned Land and Conseil, I decided to set off immediately. As we climbed higher and higher, we found ourselves surrounded by hardened, stratified lava flows.

"Look, a hive!" exclaimed Ned.

The higher we climbed, the more light filtered through the crater, and a swarm of bees had indeed built a hive in the trunk of a bush growing among the rocks. We stocked up on honey, and Ned didn't spare any of the birds that had ventured all the way out there.

Then it was time to go back to the *Nautilus*, which continued its southward journey through the Atlantic waters.

I thought the *Nautilus* would surely strike west after doubling
Cape Horn, to make its way back to the Pacific, but I was wrong.
The vessel continued to move towards the southernmost regions.
One morning, while on the surface of the water, Ned Land's
unerring eye spotted something ahead of us: a herd of baleen
whales.

"Ah, if only I were on board a whaler now!" Ned exclaimed.

"Have you ever hunted in these seas before?" I asked him.

"No, just in the northernmost seas – in the Bering and Davis
Straits."

"So you're unfamiliar with the baleen whale; up until now, you've
only ever hunted the bowhead whale, which never goes past the
warm waters of the equator," I told him.

As Ned continued to look unconvinced, I explained how whales
tend to remain in the waters they were born in and so, according
to their species, you could find them in one sea rather than
another.

"All the more reason to be on a whaler and get to know them,"
replied Ned, who couldn't take his eyes off the creatures. He was
a harpooner, after all, and the desire to hunt and to defy nature
– that is, the sea and its most powerful inhabitants – still burned
within him. Meanwhile, he told us spectacular tales of his past whale
hunts, though they seemed highly fanciful in the eyes of a naturalist.
"These animals are said to live a thousand years!" he said
enthusiastically.
"And do you know why, my dear Ned?" I asked.
"Because people say so!" the poor man answered.
So I told my companions how, when fishermen first hunted
whales four hundred years previously, these animals were much
bigger than they were today, because today they were killed
sooner, and so didn't have time to reach their full growth.
This was why they were said to have such a long life.
And while we were discussing whales, the *Nautilus* continued
its southward journey.

One morning, I spotted floating icebergs. Ned Land, who had
fished in the Arctic Sea before, was already familiar with them, but
it was the first time for Conseil and myself, and we couldn't take
our eyes off of the stunning sight. A dazzling white band stretched
as far as the eye could see towards the southern horizon, and the
differently-shaped icebergs reflected the sunlight in endless brilliant
colors. The *Nautilus* cruised between them, finding passageway
after passageway. The captain spent most of his days on the
platform, never taking his eyes off that white desert landscape until
we finally came to the great ice pack, an insurmountable obstacle
for every navigator who had come before us. But Captain Nemo
had no intention of halting his course; he wished to reach the as
yet unexplored lands that lay beyond. And so the *Nautilus* sank
beneath the surface. No longer able to pass through the ice floes,
the captain meant to go under them, even at the risk of staying
submerged for several days. The greatest difficulty, certainly, would
be resurfacing, as the sea might be frozen over. And, as the *Nautilus*
slowly attempted to rise to the surface, we soon realized just how
impossible our venture might be. As soon as it encountered a block
of ice, the submarine had to descend again, and try somewhere else.
Then one morning, after several failed attempts, we finally reached
the surface. Rushing onto the platform, I saw flocks of birds in the
air and the sea stretching into the distance.
"Are we at the South Pole?" I asked Captain Nemo excitedly.
"We'll know at noon, when we'll be able to fix our position…
if this mist clears up, that is."
When we finally sighted land, just a short distance away, we set off
in the longboat and clambered up a small ridge.
Though the vegetation seemed desolate,
there were magnificent animals
everywhere we looked: birds,
penguins, walruses, seals…

Forcing a passage through the ice seemed like an impossible feat, but

Nemo – often standing lookout himself in those days – had no intention of giving up.

The mists hadn't cleared, meanwhile, nor had the sun made an appearance although it was nearly noon. In fact, it soon began to snow, so we had to interrupt our surveying and hurry back to the *Nautilus* amid the flurries. The snowstorm lasted all night, so Conseil and I continued recording our observations from inside. By the next morning, however, the blizzard had luckily stopped tormenting the polar skies, so the *Nautilus* could advance further up the coastline. As soon as it came to a halt, we set off once more to explore these as yet uncharted territories. His temper crosser than ever, Ned Land refused, once again, to join us. Conseil and I busied ourselves classifying the marine mammals we saw all about us: seals and walruses, sea lions and elephant seals. Most of them were sleeping on the rocks or the sand. Beyond a small promontory, we observed a choir of walruses playing with each other on a vast white plain, and drew near enough to observe them closely. As it was nearly noon by then, we rejoined Captain Nemo to watch his surveying.

Noon arrived and, just like the day before, the sun didn't make an appearance. Tomorrow would be our last chance – the day after being the equinox, when the sun would disappear below the horizon for six months.

At dawn the next day, I climbed onto the platform, where I found
Captain Nemo, as restless as I was but with high hopes.
"Doesn't it look like the weather is clearing a bit, Professor
Aronnax?" he asked. "And it should improve over the next few
hours. We'll make our way ashore after breakfast to choose the
best observation post for our purposes."
The sky did seem to be clearing up, so we decided to have breakfast
at once and head for shore as soon as possible. The *Nautilus* had
traveled a few more miles during the night, so the longboat –
carrying, in addition to Conseil and myself, Captain Nemo, two
crewmen and the instruments we needed, that is a chronometer,
a spyglass and a barometer – took us to a new shore, dominated
by a rocky peak several feet high.
Captain Nemo headed for the peak, where he planned to set up his
observatory. It took us two hours to reach the summit, but we were
met by stunning views. A vast expanse of sea spread out below us,
while above us we could see the pale azure of the sky, finally clear
of clouds. The *Nautilus*, in the distance, looked like a sleeping
cetacean and, as far as the eye could see, we were surrounded
by immense, and apparently endless, shores of rocks and ice.
This time, when noon came, we could finally see the sun. And so,
precisely at twelve, observing the sun's refractions with his spyglass,
Captain Nemo solemnly called out: "The South Pole!"
He unfurled a flag with the letter "N" embroidered on it and placed
it on these lands which no man had set foot on until that day –
March 21st, 1868.

free the Nautilus with blows from our picks.

The ice surrounded us on all sides, trapping us so we couldn't float clear. Our only choice was to

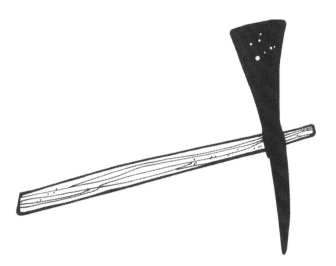

Preparations for departure began early the next morning, and the *Nautilus* soon submerged, starting its return voyage beneath the ice pack. The first day went by uneventfully, but we were awakened by a violent collision the following dawn. I rushed to the lounge, where my friends had gathered. "An iceberg has overturned, hitting the *Nautilus*, and is still under us," explained Captain Nemo. "We have to empty the tanks if we hope to get our ship floating again." Rising to the surface, the *Nautilus* was soon on its way again.

A few days later, however, we collided with another ice pack that was blocking our way. So we decided to retrace our steps, but unfortunately there were blocks of ice to the south, as well. We therefore found ourselves trapped – surrounded by great walls of ice above and below us, to the north and the south. Furthermore, we had been submerged for several days, so our oxygen supply wouldn't last much longer.

As the captain himself said, we had only one choice left: put on our diving suits and attack the walls of ice with picks. Our predicament was serious enough to require everyone's help, so my companions and I joined the crewmen. We worked in shifts, replacing each other every two hours. Whenever we reentered the *Nautilus*, we became aware of the increased heaviness of the air. Our oxygen supply was nearly exhausted and it was becoming harder to breathe. We walked around in a daze, our lips blue. So Captain Nemo decided to rely on the *Nautilus*'s ram to break through the last feet of ice. As the tanks were being filled, we heard cracking noises that told us we were moving, and the *Nautilus* abruptly began to sink into the waters! We sped ahead at full steam in the hopes of overtaking the ice pack. As I lost consciousness, dimly aware that I was about to die, I suddenly felt a breath of fresh air. The *Nautilus* had finally resurfaced.

Electric rays have flattened bodies, white on the bottom and reddish on the top, with large blue spots. Their bodies end with a caudal fin.

After having escaped from this greatest of dangers, the *Nautilus* resumed its journey. And, as we recovered our strength, we couldn't stop smiling – we were so thankful to be alive!

"But where are we going now, Professor?" asked Ned Land.

"We're finally heading north again, but it's too soon to tell if the *Nautilus* is taking us towards the Pacific or the Atlantic." The submarine traveled swiftly, at any rate, and we soon cleared the polar circle. By evening, we realized that we were heading north via the Atlantic Ocean. The next day, when the *Nautilus* surfaced, we sighted the archipelago that makes up *Tierra del Fuego* – the Land of Fire. The *Nautilus* cruised near the South American coastline for several days, at such a great speed that we soon crossed the equator. The next time the *Nautilus* resurfaced, we found ourselves just off the Amazon River. We stayed afloat for a few days, while the crew devoted itself to fishing.

The *Nautilus*'s fishing nets brought on board a multitude of fascinating fish that I was eager to classify, including one that poor Conseil won't forget in a hurry!

"Aaaahhh, Master! Help, Master, please help me!" he cried, his legs in the air.

He had touched an electric ray caught in one of the nets we hauled in – an extremely dangerous creature.

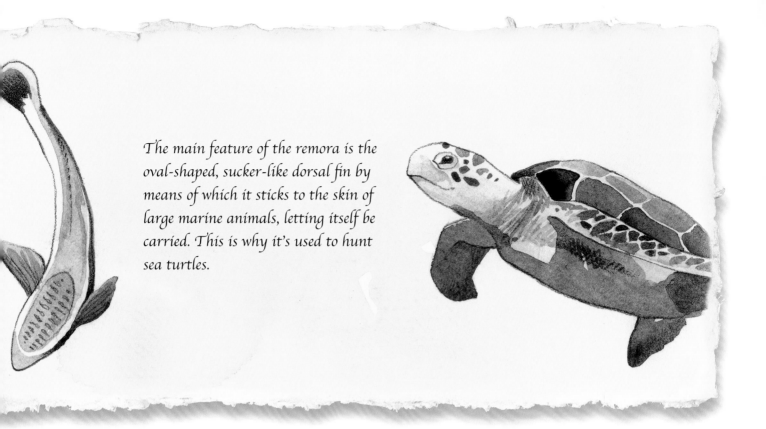

The main feature of the remora is the oval-shaped, sucker-like dorsal fin by means of which it sticks to the skin of large marine animals, letting itself be carried. This is why it's used to hunt sea turtles.

Shaped like a disk, it had a docked tail and flattened body, white on the bottom and red on the top, with large blue spots. When it's in the water, it can electrocute people from several feet away, so great is its electric power. The nets also hauled in some bizarre fish whose heads were formed by an oval-shaped slab, which is the peculiarity of the remora. Consisting of crosswise plates of moveable cartilage, between which the animals can create a vacuum, it creates a suction cup that allows them stick to other fish and be carried along. Once the fishing was done, the *Nautilus* drew nearer to the coast, where a number of sea turtles were sleeping.

We decided to use the suckerfish to capture a few valuable specimens, and it proved a good idea – they fastened easily onto the turtles' shells, allowing us to hoist the valuable animals on board.

The *Nautilus* then took to the high seas, submerging once more as it left the Amazon River behind.

We kept veering away from the Mexican coast, and Ned Land – who was still hoping to escape from the *Nautilus* – had to resign himself to his fate once more.

Meanwhile, Captain Nemo rarely put in an appearance, and looked grimmer and grimmer the few times I saw him.

We began to rise towards the surface after several days, and I conjectured us to be within range of the archipelago of the Bahamas. We sighted a series of underwater cliffs among which there were several dark caverns. Who knew what was hidden in their depths…

It was Ned who drew our attention to a great tangle in the midst of the seaweed.

"These are caverns inhabited by giant squid! I wonder if we'll happen to see any of these monsters," I said. Conseil couldn't take his eyes off the caverns, hoping to catch a glimpse of the giant squid he had heard so much about, creatures violent and strong enough to sink a ship.

"Professor, do you truly believe that such animals exist?" asked Ned.

"I've seen one! In a painting in a church…" said Conseil.

"There you have it, then," chuckled Ned.

"But, Master, isn't it true that the giant squid is at least twenty feet long, with eight quivering tentacles on its head, tiny eyes and a mouth that resembles a parrot's beak, but of enormous size?

"That's correct, Conseil."

As he pointed to the glass panels, we turned and gave shouts of fear. The *Nautilus* was surrounded by eight giant squid, who had wrapped their long tentacles around it. As the submarine came to an abrupt halt, Captain Nemo entered the lounge.

"We're going to rise to the surface and fight these monsters face to face; their tentacles seem to have jammed the *Nautilus*'s propeller."

"I'll help you, Captain, if I may," said Ned Land.

Conseil and I witnessed the scene.

The crewmen, Ned Land and Captain Nemo himself managed
to set the *Nautilus* free by chopping off the tentacles with their
axes. Tragically, however, one of the seamen was snatched by
a tentacle, and nothing could be done to save him.

After a terrifying battle, the giant squid finally retreated, and
we set off once more, greatly saddened by our loss.

Captain Nemo retired to his stateroom, and for ten days the
Nautilus seemed to navigate at random, floating aimlessly on
the water. It was only on the tenth day that the *Nautilus* finally
resumed its northbound coast, following the Gulf Stream – a
river that flows through the middle of the Atlantic. Following
the current, we soon approached an area known for the terrible
cyclones and tornadoes caused by the Gulf Stream.

The skies became more and more threatening as we went on,
the storm finally bursting as the *Nautilus* was a few miles off the
coast of New York. Instead of facing this terrible squall from
fathoms below, Captain Nemo chose to stay on the surface of
the water and face it head-on. We were buffeted and tossed
about by the wind and the hurricane, until it became impossible
to stand upright inside the *Nautilus*. That was when Captain
Nemo finally gave orders to descend, and we found tranquility
once more.

The storm had blown us away from New York, and we were now heading in a northeasterly direction. After cruising along the underwater Banks of Newfoundland, we headed east again, finally reaching the coast of Ireland. Much to my surprise, however, the *Nautilus* then headed back south, to the European seas and the lowermost tip of England. For the next few days, the *Nautilus* outlined a series of circles on the surface of the waters, as if it were looking for a specific spot in the ocean. And so it was, because when we finally submerged and the panels opened, I saw the remains of a wrecked ship. Observing it closely, I noticed that it was still upright, though the masts were gone. It had surely sunk long ago; but what ship was this, and why had Captain Nemo been searching for it?

As if he had read my mind, the captain explained that it was the wreckage of the *Vengeur*, and I remembered how that famous French vessel had preferred to sink rather than surrender after a heroic battle against the English fleet.

We had no sooner returned to the surface than I heard an explosion, so I rushed to the platform, where Conseil and Ned had already gathered. Together, we watched a ship slowly approaching the *Nautilus*.

"It was a cannon going off, Professor, from that warship out there."

A second shot was fired at us, but the shell landed in the sea, spraying us with water.

That's when I realized the truth: when the *Abraham Lincoln* had attacked the *Nautilus*, Commander Farragut had undoubtedly realized that the monstrous narwhal was, in fact, a submarine, so several ships must now be chasing after it.

Looking distraught, Captain Nemo joined us on the platform.

"Get below, you and your companions!" he shouted at me.

"Do you mean to attack that ship, Captain?" I asked.

"I'm going to sink it, Professor!"

84

His face distorted with rage, Captain Nemo climbed onto the

platform, furiously shaking his fist, to see who had dared to attack the Nautilus.

"You can't be serious!" I retorted.

But Captain Nemo, more furious than I had ever seen him, had no intention of leaving the battlefield. So Conseil, Ned and I had no choice but to return to our cabins.

As I was going below, I heard the captain shouting at the mysterious ship, his voice quivering with indescribable hatred and rage.

"Come closer, you useless vessel, and shoot your cannons at me! But you'll be no match for the *Nautilus* and its mighty steel ram! Nor will you perish here, where one of the most glorious ships in history lies! You don't deserve to mingle with the wreckage of the *Vengeur*!

The realization that the captain would show the ship no mercy, and the thought of helplessly witnessing the massacre while I was trapped inside the *Nautilus*, caused me great anguish.

Thus Ned Land, Conseil and I decided to escape during the night, and swim towards the other ship when it had come close enough; we preferred to sink with her than stay to witness Captain Nemo's terrible revenge.

But alas! At dawn, when the time had come to escape, Captain Nemo ordered the hatches to be closed, and the *Nautilus* submerged a few feet below the surface. We had no way out. Then – and only then – I finally realized why the captain had locked us in our cell and put us to sleep, that long-ago night in the middle of the Indian Ocean. He must have been preparing to take his revenge on another ship that was after the *Nautilus*. And that wounded seaman must have been hurt in a similar battle.

We felt the *Nautilus*'s speed increase noticeably, as if it were gathering momentum, then heard the sound of its steel ram tearing through the vessel.

It was a terrible noise, and I would have given anything to never have heard it. I covered my ears with a shout, but this didn't make it any less unbearable. Unable to stand it any longer, I rushed out of my stateroom and into the lounge. Captain Nemo was there, cruelly silent, staring through the glass panels at the scene unfolding before our eyes.

Following his gaze, I saw an enormous mass sinking towards
the bottom of the sea as the *Nautilus* slowly followed its descent.
A sudden eruption, caused by the compressed air, sent all the decks
flying, and the explosion caused the *Nautilus* to swerve from its
course. Afterwards, the ship sank even more swiftly, dragging all
it carried down with it – cannons, masts, iron timbers. And men.
When it was all over, Captain Nemo opened the door to his
stateroom and entered without closing it behind him.
I never took my eyes off him, following his every movement.
Hanging on the wall, above the portraits of his heroes, I spied
the portrait of a young woman and two little children.
Kneeling before the portrait, the captain began to sob.

whirpool from which nothing has ever been known to escape.

The Maelstrom is the most dangerous area off the Norwegian coast! Here the waters form a

I reentered my stateroom, where Ned and Conseil were waiting for me. Silence reigned throughout the *Nautilus*. The sights I had seen still filled me with horror. As soon as the electric lights came back on, I went into the lounge to mark our position on the chart; we were headed towards the northernmost seas at incalculable speed. From that day forward, I could no longer tell what coasts we visited, what seas we crossed. I lost track of time, because the ship's clocks had stopped, although I imagine that the *Nautilus*'s haphazard course continued for about twenty days. We mostly traveled under water, and when the *Nautilus* would rise to the surface for air, its hatches would open and close almost immediately. Then one morning, Ned came to me and said: "I've sighted land, Professor, not so far off. We'll escape tonight!"

This time I was in complete agreement with Ned, although the sea was rough and the wind was blowing hard.

I returned to the lounge, a mass of contradictions. I would have liked to see Captain Nemo one last time but, still shaken by the unspeakable horrors I had watched him commit, I also dreaded the thought of seeing him. The hour came at long last. From my stateroom, I could hear the chords of the organ, which meant that Captain Nemo was surely in the lounge, which I had to cross. Fearing the worst, I opened the lounge door to find the room in darkness, and I realized that Captain Nemo wouldn't notice me. As I left the room, I heard him sobbing, and he gasped out these words: "Oh, God! Enough, enough!"

I rushed to join my companions, and we had just climbed into the longboat when we heard a sudden commotion on the platform. "Maelstrom! Maelstrom!" the crewmen were yelling. The most frightening word we could have imagined, shouted out in fear and desperation. My heart stood still, and I could hardly breathe. The Maelstrom! That great and fearsome whirlpool!

This meant that the *Nautilus* found itself in the most dangerous area off the Norwegian coast, at the very moment when we planned to make our escape in the frail longboat.

In this area, the waters confined between the Faroe and Lofoten islands rush out with indescribable violence, forming a dangerous vortex from which no ship has ever been known to escape. Known as "the ocean's navel", this whirlpool can suck down anything that happens by, no matter the size: ships, whales, bears... Steered by a captain who seemed to have lost his way after recent traumatic events, the *Nautilus* had accidentally ended up in this whirlpool and was now sweeping around in a spiral that grew smaller and smaller. The longboat, still attached to the side of the *Nautilus*, was also carried around at a dizzying speed. Drenched in a cold sweat, our nerves numb, we could no longer hear our heartbeats. All we could hear was the deafening roar of waves crashing against rocks and the sound of the *Nautilus* swirling around in the treacherous whirlpool.

The longboat was rocking violently, and Conseil, Ned and I were tossed from one side to the other, unable to keep our balance in that senseless, ceaseless movement. We were

paralyzed by fear, gripped by terror, and unable to think clearly…
Although what was there to think about?!

Only Ned, brave and fearless as his job had taught him to be,
kept spurring us on.

"We've got to hold on tight, and stay attached to the *Nautilus*!" he kept
screaming like one possessed. I could hear his voice, a blend of desperation
and strength, telling us to screw the nuts and bolts back down.
But no sooner had he got the words out than we heard a terrible
cracking sound, as if something had broken.

The last bolts gave way, and our longboat was hurled like a spear
into the midst of the vortex. The last thing I remember before I lost
consciousness was striking my head against an iron timber.

I'm unable to say what else happened that night, nor how our
longboat managed to escape the powerful Maelstrom whirpool.
I have no idea how we managed to survive, Conseil, Ned and I.
But we did survive, and found ourselves lying in a fisherman's hut
on one of the Lofoten Islands when we regained consciousness.
This fisherman had found us cast up on the beach,
unconscious, and had brought us to his hut to look after us.
We were overjoyed to find ourselves alive, although we had
no memory of the events of that terrible night.

There is no question of returning to France for the moment, as roads between northern and southern Norway are not well developed. We have to wait for the arrival of a steamboat that provides bimonthly service to and from North Cape.
So we are still among these good folks who saved our lives, and it is here that I'm reading my journal to relive our adventures. It is a faithful account of a journey through the depths of the oceans, as incredible as it is true.
While I do wonder if anyone will believe me, I know that, ultimately, it doesn't matter.
All that truly matters is that in these ten months I've traveled twenty thousand leagues under the sea, on an underwater tour of the world that has shown me countless wonders – usually inaccessible to mankind – across the Pacific and the Indian Ocean, the Red Sea and the Mediterranean, the Atlantic and, last but not least, the southernmost and northernmost seas!
Yet I often wonder what happened to the *Nautilus*. Did it escape the Maelstrom? Is Captain Nemo still alive? Has he stopped attacking other ships to relieve his thirst for vengeance?
I recall that he was writing a manuscript that told his life story, as well as detailing the discoveries he had made throughout his sea voyage. He kept it in a special, waterproof casket, and one

day told me that he had given orders that the last man left
on board the *Nautilus* was to throw it into the waves.
Who knows if this came to pass, and if we shall ever have
the chance to read it…
I like to imagine that Captain Nemo is still alive, and I hope that
the wonders of the underwater world may someday alleviate his
grief, leading him to the peace he is looking for.
And I also like to imagine that, to the question asked over a
thousand years ago – *Who can fathom the soundless depths?* – only
two men have earned the right to answer: Captain Nemo and I.

The Voyage of

North
America

Atlantic
Ocean

Pacific
Ocean

South
America

Antarctic
Ocean

Francesca Rossi

Born in 1983, she graduated from the International School of Comics in Florence. She publishes illustrated books with various Italian publishers and does drawings for covers and posters. In addition to illustrating, she offers educational workshops in schools and libraries, and creates and decorates ceramic art. In the last few years Rossi has illustrated, with enthusiasm and creativity, several books for White Star Kids, such as "Around the World in Eighty Days", "Little Woman" and "Gulliver's Travels" in the same series of this book.

Text adaptation **Emma Altomare**
(Contextus Srl, Pavia)

Graphic layout **Paola Piacco**

White Star Kids® is a registered trademark property of White Star s.r.l.

© 2017 White Star s.r.l.
Piazzale Luigi Cadorna, 6 - 20123 Milan, Italy
www.whitestar.it

Translation and editing: Contextus Srl, Pavia, Italy (Daniela Innocenti)

ISBN 978-88-544-1183-8
1 2 3 4 5 6 21 20 19 18 17

Printed in China